For Potato

D.P.

MR. SWEET POTATO - A Dapper Kitty from the City
ISBN: 978-1-954277-19-9

Text © 2023 Dimitria Parisis Phillips
Illustrations © 2023 Doaly
All rights reserved.
Manufactured by Regent Publishing Services Ltd. Printed in Shenzhen, China.

This book, or any portion thereof, may not be reproduced or used in any manner without
the express written permission of the publisher, except for the use
of brief quotation in book reviews.

This book was published by JCP Strategies in partnership with McSea Books 2023
To connect visit: https://potatosworld.co or www.mcseabooks.com

MR. SWEET POTATO

A DAPPER KITTY FROM THE CITY

Written by Dimitria Parisis Phillips - Illustrated by Doaly

Meet Mr. Sweet Potato
— A Dapper Kitty from the City.

Start spreading the news
because today is his big special day…

At 7:00 a.m., it's time for Mr. Sweet Potato's morning routine.

There's a rumor that all kitties despise water,
but Mr. Sweet Potato is different.

He washes behind his ears
and in between his paws,

taking extra care
not to miss a spot.

At 7:30 a.m., it's time to pick a bow tie from
Mr. Sweet Potato's beautiful collection.
This special day calls for his favorite one!

During breakfast, Pigeon stops by to deliver the news.

"Good morning!" coos Pigeon.

"The weather is purrrrfect for your big special day!
No need for an umbrella, and traffic is light."

"Excellent!" meows Mr. Sweet Potato.

"Greetings, Ramone." he says to the doorman.

"Good day, Mr. Sweet Potato! You are up bright and early. Are you excited for your big special day?"

"I certainly am, and I hope to see you there!"

BEEP! BEEP!
Up pulls George in his taxicab.

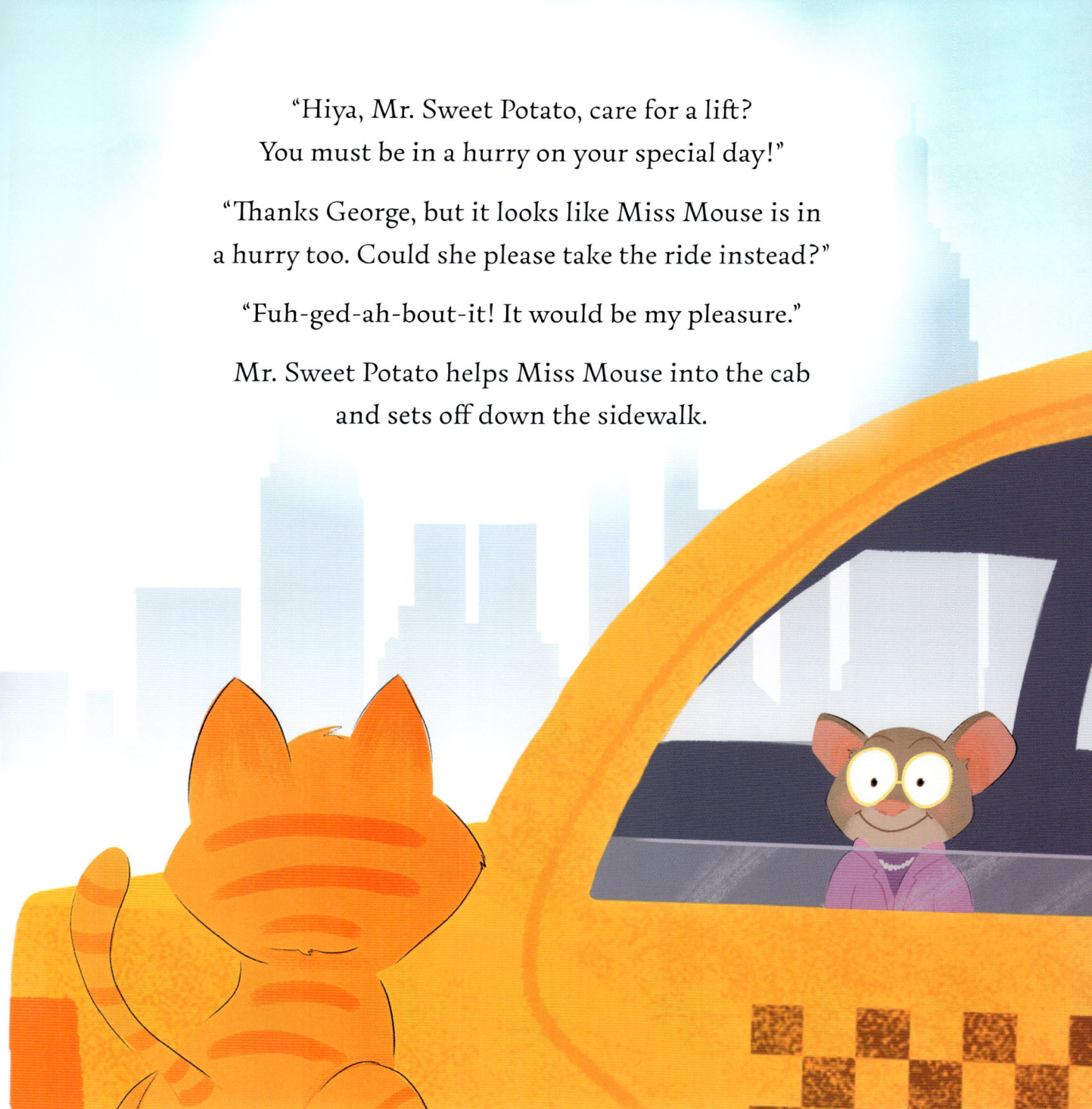

"Hiya, Mr. Sweet Potato, care for a lift? You must be in a hurry on your special day!"

"Thanks George, but it looks like Miss Mouse is in a hurry too. Could she please take the ride instead?"

"Fuh-ged-ah-bout-it! It would be my pleasure."

Mr. Sweet Potato helps Miss Mouse into the cab and sets off down the sidewalk.

On his way, Mr. Sweet Potato hears a sensational melody.

"Bears! Your music is marvelous!" he cheers,
as he places a coin in their bag.

At 9:00 a.m., Mr. Sweet Potato passes the cheese shop and notices something strange.

"Tony, what are you doing? Shouldn't your cheese shop be open by now?"

"Oh, hi, Mr. Sweet Potato. I'm locked out of my shop! I dropped the key, and now it's lost."

"Meowzah! Let's look together!"

"Oh no, I don't want to make you late on your big special day."

But Mr. Sweet Potato presses his furry face close to the ground, looks all around, and after a little while, he finds the key. Hurray!

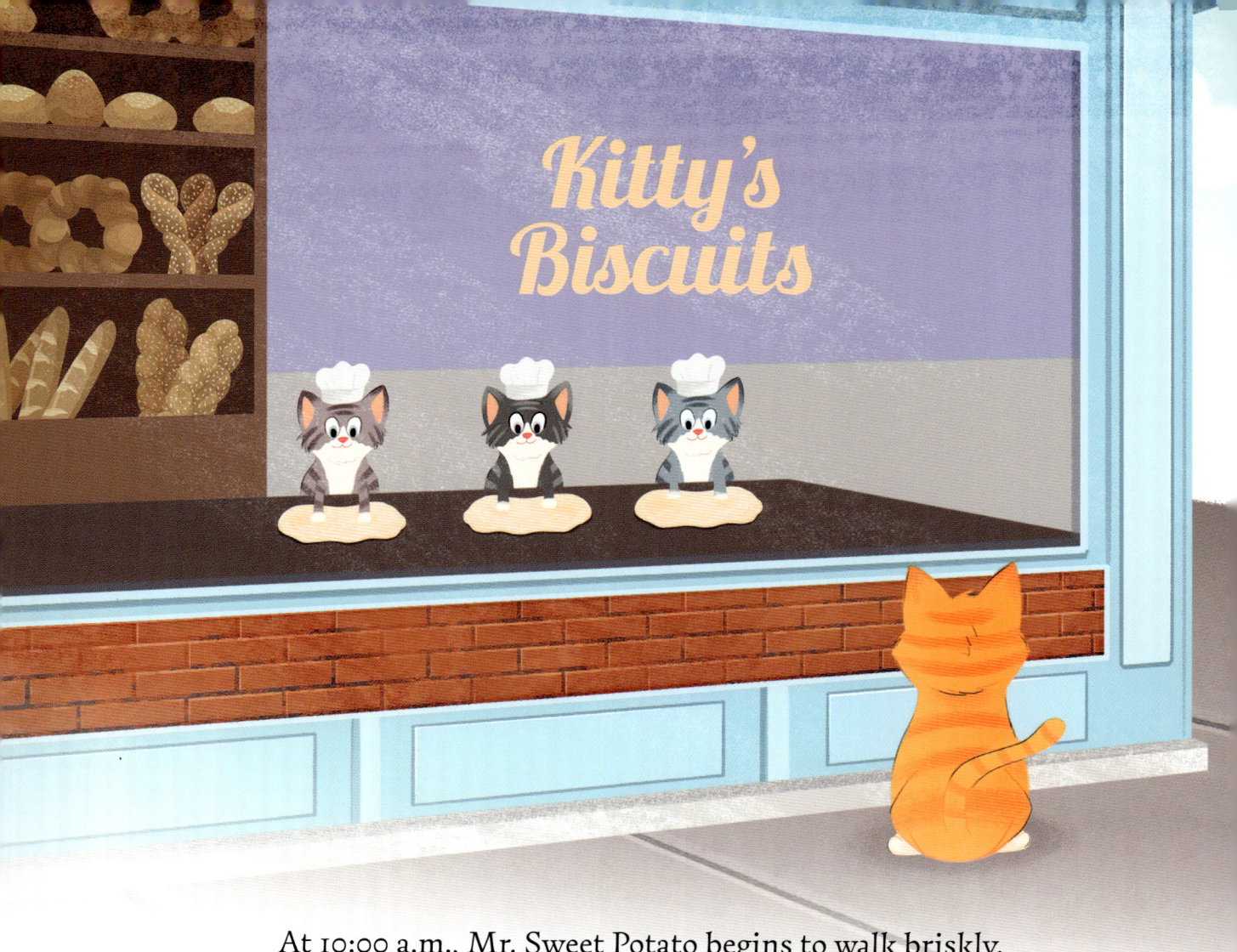

At 10:00 a.m., Mr. Sweet Potato begins to walk briskly.

"Oh no, oh no, oh no! Something's just not right!" Kitty shouts from the bakery.

"What's the matter?" Mr. Sweet Potato asks.

"These biscuits aren't rising properly," replies Kitty. "I just don't know what to do."

Mr. Sweet Potato knows he's late, but he decides to make another stop to help.

"Let me share my recipe with you!" he says.

At 11:15 a.m., Mr. Sweet Potato has almost arrived at his destination. He stops to take a sniff of Flo's beautiful flowers when he hears a gigantic noise!

THUD, CRASH, SPLAT!

"Flo, are you okay?" asks Mr. Sweet Potato.

"Oh, Mr. Sweet Potato! My flower arrangements have fallen. Ugh, what a mess!"

Mr. Sweet Potato thinks for a moment. If he helps his friend Flo, he will most certainly be very late for his big special day. What should he do? Flo is his friend and friends deserve help. Mr. Sweet Potato begins picking up flowers, and just like that, his favorite bow tie tears on a thorn. Oh no!

Mr. Sweet Potato looks down at his tie, and his eyes begin to well with tears.

Now he's not only very, very late, but very, very dirty, and he's wearing a very, very, very ripped bow tie. What a cat-astrophe!

"Help me-ow!" cries Mr. Sweet Potato.

Even though it's half past late, and he's quite the mess,
Mr. Sweet Potato finally makes it to his big special day…

It's the grand opening of his cafe, Potato's Place!
And Mr. Sweet Potato cannot believe his eyes.
What a large crowd!

Pigeon has flown flyers all throughout the city. George gave all the guests a lift. The bears set the mood with wonderful tunes. Tony brought cheese for all the sandwiches. Kitty supplied her famous biscuits. Flo arranged beautiful, fragrant flowers for the decor. Last, but not least, Penguin the Tailor came to the rescue to fix Mr. Sweet Potato's bow tie!

As Penguin works on mending the tattered tie, Mr. Sweet Potato borrows Penguin's handkerchief to clean his fur.

"Penguin, how did you know that I needed your help?"

"Why Flo told me!" Penguin said.

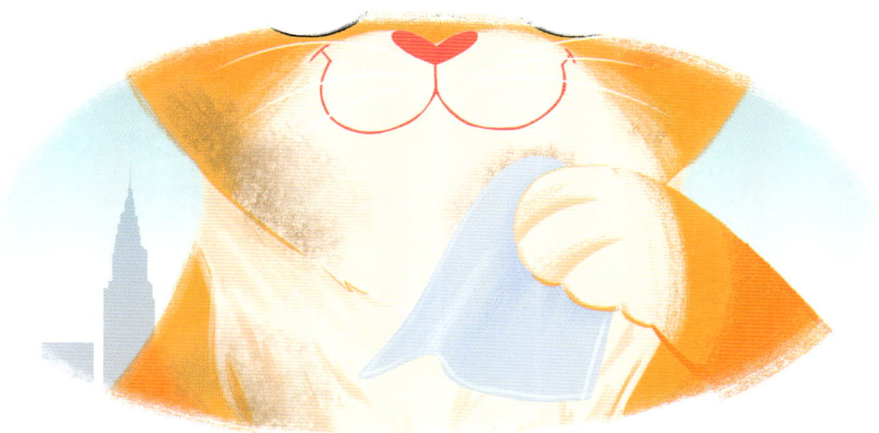

Mr. Sweet Potato was so moved by his friends' generosity. He flashed a giant smile from ear to ear! All of the friends he had helped along the way came together to help make his special day spectacular! And just like that, our Dapper Kitty from the city learns a wonderful lesson…

Potato, fondly known as Mr. Sweet Potato, was the bow-tie-loving Dapper Kitty from New York City. He was fostered by Beth Stern in 2015 through the North Shore Animal League America and was quickly adopted by Dimitria Parisis. His curious, loving, and humorous personality inspired Dimitria to write this book.

Unfortunately, Potato passed away in 2022 due to health complications. His essence lives on through this book. In honor of Potato's rescue story, we pledge to donate a portion of proceeds to cats and kittens in need.

MEET THE CREATORS

Dimitria Parisis is a native New Yorker and was living in Manhattan when she adopted Potato. Potato's adorable antics paired with Dimitria's passion to teach children self empowerment and transformation through sharing inspired her to write this book. She lives in West Palm Beach, Florida with her husband Coby and their rescue dog Charlie.

Doaly is a UK-based graphic designer and digital illustrator with a passion for storytelling. His work is characterized by his bold conceptual approach to illustration and his ability to adapt his style to be most sympathetic to the subject matter.

Over the years he has created artwork for a wide range of clients including the BBC, Disney, Pixar and Marvel. He is also active on the pop culture gallery scene and has created official artwork for properties including Spider-Man, Star Wars and Southpark.

For more information and merchandise please visit www.potatosplace.com